Celebrate Halloween

Other titles in the *Celebrate Holidays* series

Celebrate Chinese New Year
ISBN 0-7660-2577-2

◆

Celebrate Cinco de Mayo
ISBN 0-7660-2579-9

◆

Celebrate Columbus Day
ISBN 0-7660-2580-2

◆

Celebrate Halloween
ISBN 0-7660-2491-1

◆

Celebrate Martin Luther King, Jr., Day
ISBN 0-7660-2492-X

◆

Celebrate St. Patrick's Day
ISBN 0-7660-2581-0

◆

Celebrate Thanksgiving Day
ISBN 0-7660-2578-0

Celebrate Halloween

Wendy Mass

These trick-or-treaters grab some candy.

Enslow Publishers, Inc.
40 Industrial Road
Box 398
Berkeley Heights, NJ 07922
USA

http://www.enslow.com

For Linda, Ursula, and Mika Raedisch.
May all your Halloweens be full of wonder and magic.

Library of Congress Cataloging-in-Publication Data

Mass, Wendy, 1967–
   Celebrate Halloween / Wendy Mass.
     p. cm. — (Celebrate holidays)
   Includes bibliographical references and index.
   ISBN 0-7660-2491-1
     1. Halloween—Juvenile literature. I. Title. II. Series.
   GT4965.M264 2006
   394.2646—dc22

                           2005028109

Printed in the United States of America

10 9 8 7 6 5 4 3 2 1

To Our Readers: We have done our best to make sure all Internet Addresses in this book were active and appropriate when we went to press. However, the author and the publisher have no control over and assume no liability for the material available on those Internet sites or on other Web sites they may link to. Any comments or suggestions can be sent by e-mail to comments@ enslow.com or to the address on the back cover.

Every effort has been made to locate all copyright holders of material used in this book. If any errors or omissions have occurred, corrections will be made in future editions of this book.

CONTENTS

The Mysterious Tale of the Jack-O'-Lantern

An old Irish legend tells of a man named Jack, who lived hundreds of years ago. Jack was not a very nice person. He liked to play tricks on everyone. One day it was time for the Devil to take Jack's soul to hell. The Devil and Jack walked together on a dirt road, but Jack had no plans to accompany the Devil back home. He waited for the perfect chance to trick the Devil.

He got his chance as they approached an apple tree. "Look," Jack said, pointing at the crisp apples. "Don't they look delicious? Wouldn't they be wonderful for the long trip?"

The Devil agreed that they did look ripe and red and juicy. He climbed up the tree to pick a few. Jack took this moment to carve a cross into the bark with his pocketknife. When the Devil saw this, he realized he was trapped. He could not get down from the tree.

Jack said, "I'll let you down, if you promise not to make me go to hell with you. Ever."

The Devil had no choice but to agree. Years later, Jack died. His soul went up to heaven, but he was not allowed in. He had not been a good person and did not deserve to go to heaven. Jack had no choice but to travel to hell. But the Devil kept his promise and would not allow Jack in.

"Where am I supposed to go?" Jack whined. "Just wander between heaven and hell? It is so dark here."

The Devil threw Jack a burning ember from the fires of hell so he could see better. Jack had a turnip in his pocket that he had stolen before he died. He hollowed it out and stuck the ember inside. He used this as a lantern to guide his way.

Pumpkins can be carved in many different ways to create a jack-o'-lantern.

Ever since then, the Irish people hollowed out all kinds of vegetables, including potatoes and beets, and put lights in them. They used these "lanterns" to keep evil spirits away from their homes. When the Irish came to America, they brought this tradition with them. They soon realized that a pumpkin was very easy to carve, and the jack o'-lantern, as we know it today, was born.

The History of Halloween

The word *Halloween* means "the evening before All Hallows' or All Saints' Day," a Christian holiday. But you do not have to be Christian to celebrate Halloween. In fact, people have been celebrating something like Halloween since long before the coming of Christianity. The holiday as we know it had its roots thousands of years ago and thousands of miles away, in Europe.

Fall is harvest season in Europe, as it is in America, and a good harvest would ensure the people would be fed for another year. If the harvest was bad, many people might not survive another year. This was also the time of year that ancient Europeans used to remember and pray for the dead. Our present-day Halloween borrows from both of these traditions.

Samhain

Halloween reportedly began with the Celts, an ancient European people whose descendants include the Irish, Welsh, and Scottish people of today. The ancient Irish people observed two important festivals each year. At Beltane, they celebrated the beginning of spring and warm weather. Beltane took place around May 1 to celebrate the arrival of the warm weather, when the herds could be released out into the fields again to graze. The festival of Samhain (pronounced sow-an) marked the end of summer and the beginning of the new year.[1]

Samhain was celebrated on November 1, when the newly harvested food was stored away and both people and animals settled down for the long winter. The night of Samhain was the boundary between summer and winter, the old year and the new year. It was also believed to be the boundary between the world of the living and the world of the dead.[2]

Facts About the Druids

The Druids were the educated class among the Celts, an ancient European people. They were priests, judges, and lawmakers. They led religious ceremonies, settled legal conflicts, and acted as leaders and advisers.

Their religion was Druidism, which involved the worship of many gods. They believed that the soul was immortal and entered a new body after death. The Druids sacrificed animals, and possibly people, as part of religious ceremonies. The religion died after the Celts became Christians in the 400s and 500s.

Today, several groups in the United Kingdom and Ireland practice ancient Druidism as they believe it was practiced in ancient times, even holding Druid festivals at the beginning of spring, summer, autumn, and winter.

One of the Irish legends surrounding Samhain says that on this day everyone put out his home hearth fire. To light them again, people went to the great fire the Druids had built at Tara, home of the Irish kings.[3] One reason the Druids built the new fire, or need-fire as they called it, may have been to encourage the sun to burn brightly again as it had during the long days of summer.[4] Relighting their home fires from the Druids' need-fire was the ancient Celts' way of starting fresh and getting the year off to a good start.

The Celts also believed that on this night, the closeness of the spirit world made it easier to predict the future.[5] People believed they could tell fortunes by casting stones into the roaring fires they built on the hilltops. They also expected visits from their dead relatives, for wandering souls were believed to find their way home at this time of year.

The Ancient Romans

According to legend, the city-state of Rome was founded on seven hills by twin brothers Romulus and Remus in 753 B.C. Over the course of twelve centuries, Rome grew to become arguably the greatest empire in history before its collapse. At its high point, Rome controlled about half of Europe, a majority of the Middle East, and the north coast of Africa.

During the fifth century A.D., the western part of the empire broke off into independent kingdoms. In A.D. 476 the eastern part of the empire came to be known as the Byzantine Empire, with its capital in Constantinople, which is in modern-day Turkey.

Ancient Rome revolutionized the development of law, art, war literature, architecture, and language.

To welcome their departed loved ones, the living left out gifts of food and water. They also hoped that once they had eaten, the ghosts would go away again without causing any trouble.[6] In addition to ghosts, witches and "hobgoblins" [supernatural creatures] were supposed to be roaming around on Samhain.[7]

One might think of Samhain as the great-grandfather of today's Halloween. But Halloween as it is celebrated today contains bits and pieces of other festivals as well. When the Romans invaded Britain around A.D. 43, they brought their own festivals with them. Some of the Roman traditions mingled with those of the Celts.

Pomona, Parentalia, and Lemuria

We likely have the Roman goddess Pomona to thank for the apple's place beside the jack-o'-lantern as a symbol of Halloween. Pomona was the goddess of the orchards and her festival was held on November 1. Feasts of fruit and nuts were given in her honor to ensure a good harvest.

At another Roman festival called Parentalia, families honored their dead by leaving treats like milk and honey on their graves. It was a quiet time of feasting and reflection. And at the three-day festival of Lemuria, the Romans acted out rituals to protect themselves against harmful ghosts—they threw black beans at them as gifts so the ghosts would not carry off the living.[8]

Although Parentalia was celebrated in February and Lemuria in May, these festivals of the dead came to live on in Halloween.

Hallowtide

When the Romans and the Celts converted to Christianity, the Church wanted them to stop following the old pagan, or non-Christian, traditions. But the Church soon figured out that it was easier to create new Christian festivals from the pagan ones.

So, a new holiday was created: the Feast of All Saints. At first, the Feast of All Saints was celebrated on different dates in different places. Then, in 837, Pope Gregory IV ordered everybody to celebrate it on November 1, the same day as the old Samhain and Pomona. All Souls' Day, a holiday to honor the Christian dead, was originally held in the spring, about the same time as the old Beltane and Lemuria. By the early Middle Ages, however, it was being celebrated on November 2. Together, the two new holidays and the evening before them became known as Hallowtide, meaning "holy time."[9]

The Church of England

Christianity was brought to England by the Romans in the first or second century A.D. The English worshipped at Roman Catholic Churches, with the Pope having more power than the kings. Then in 1533, England's King Henry VIII wanted to annul his marriage to Katharine of Aragon, but the Pope would not allow it. King Henry decided to break with the Roman Catholic Church, and formed his own church—the Church of England.

For a few decades, the new church was a lot like the old one. The followers of the Church of England are called "Anglicans," and their traditions lay somewhere between Protestant and Catholic.

In 1534, King Henry VIII made himself head of the English Church so that he would not have to abide by the rules of the pope. Now that England was separate from the Catholic Church, the people of England were no longer supposed to observe the Catholic holidays.[10] But in Ireland, which was not under the king's jurisdiction, the people remained Catholic and continued to light bonfires as in ancient times and to go "souling" at Hallowtide.

Souling was a little bit like our modern trick-or-treating. It was also a link to the older tradition of putting out food for the dead at Samhain. The poorer residents of a village went from door to door and promised to pray for the dead in return for a "soul cake" made of oatmeal and molasses.[11] To light their way, they carried lanterns carved from turnips. The candles inside the turnips stood for the souls trapped between heaven and hell.[12]

In Ireland's County Cork, young men paraded through the streets on All Hallows' Day, asking for gifts in the name of Muck Olla, a boar from Irish legend. The leader of the parade dressed in white and wore a horse's head, perhaps because horses were sacred to the ancient Celtic sun god.[13] The other men blew on cows' horns so everyone would know they were coming. Those who gave out food and drink were promised good luck. Those who did not could expect the opposite.[14]

Guy Fawkes Day

Even though it was officially not allowed, souling continued in some parts of England. Then, in 1605, an important event occurred that helped the English create a new tradition to replace the forbidden ones of Hallowtide.

On November 5, a Catholic Englishman named Guy Fawkes was one of a group of men who tried to blow up the Houses of Parliament. Fawkes was caught with barrels of gunpowder and was the first

Guy Fawkes and the Gunpowder Plot

Guy Fawkes was born in England in 1570. Originally a Protestant, he converted to Catholicism around the age of sixteen. In 1592 he left England for the Netherlands where he served with the Catholic armies of Spain against the Protestant Dutch. A religious man, Fawkes was frustrated by the persecution Catholics received from the Protestant King James I of England.

Fawkes was recruited to join a plot to blow up Westminster Palace during the formal opening session of Parliament in 1605. If the plot was successful, the conspirators would kill the King, his family, the members of Parliament's House of Lords and House of Commons, and most of the Protestant aristocracy. The idea was that this would help to return Roman Catholicism as the dominant religion of England.

The conspirators were able to rent a room in the cellar beneath the House of Lords, in which they hid eighteen hundred pounds of gunpowder under iron bars and wood.

However, the plan was discovered. Fawkes and his fellow conspirators were caught and executed.

In Ireland, there are mysterious rock formations
that may have been built by ancient Druids.

one captured (and later killed). To celebrate the foiled attempt on the life of their king, the people of England set off fireworks. It became a tradition that on November 4 children built straw effigies, or likenesses, of Guy Fawkes. They chanted the rhyme below and begged for pennies so they could buy fireworks. The next day they set off the fireworks and threw their "guys" on a bonfire.

> Remember, Remember!
> The fifth of November,
> The Gunpowder treason and plot;
> There is no reason
> Why the Gunpowder treason
> Should ever be forgot![15]

Guy Fawkes Day was still celebrated by the English who settled colonial America. Begging "a penny for the Guy," like souling, had a long-lasting influence on the current tradition of trick-or-treating.[16]

Fortune-telling

While today we go trick-or-treating and bob for apples just for fun, these activities had different meanings in earlier times. From the pre-Christian Samhain into the last century, fortune-telling was an important part of Halloween. In England, it

Halloween bonfires were used as fortune-telling tools many years ago in England.

was believed that a woman born on Halloween could see into the future.[17] In Wales, each family member dropped a stone into the Halloween bonfire. If your stone was missing in the morning, you were sure to die before next Halloween.[18] In one part of England, candles or torches were carried through the hills to drive away witches. If your candle was not blown out, you would be safe from witches for a whole year.[19]

Halloween was also the time when a young woman could find out whom she was going to marry. One way to do this was for the girl to peel an apple round and round in one long spiral, then throw the peel over her shoulder. When the peel landed, the girl believed, it would form the initials of the man she was going to marry. She could also throw a ball of yarn out the window at midnight. Whoever picked it up would marry her. A spookier way of finding her future husband was to hold a candle up to a mirror, again at midnight on Halloween. The face of the man in question was supposed to appear over the young woman's shoulder.[20]

What if those ancient Celts, dancing around their bonfires, had been able to see really far into the future and glimpse today's trick-or-treaters and school costume parades? Would they have noticed any connection between Samhain and Halloween?

We know how the Romans brought their festivals to ancient Britain and how Pomona, Parentalia, and Lemuria mingled with the traditions of the Celts already living there. When the Irish, Scottish, and English came to America, they brought some of these mingled traditions with them.

The Cultural Significance of Halloween

Halloween as it is known in America today—with costumes, candy, and parades—did not really exist until the 1930s. In fact, it is not until the early 1900s that we even find anything like trick-or-treating happening in the United States—and not always in October.

The Ragamuffins

In the early 1900s, in New York City, children started pulling on simple, homemade costumes and begging door to door. But these ragamuffins, as they were known, did not go out at Halloween—they dressed up for Thanksgiving as a way of continuing the Guy Fawkes celebration. Instead of "Trick or treat!" they called out "Anything for Thanksgiving?"[1]

New York City tried to discourage the custom of Thanksgiving begging. In 1924, they got some help from the new Macy's Thanksgiving Parade. Upstaged by the fancy floats and huge balloons, the ragamuffins gave up dressing up for Thanksgiving—and started dressing up for Halloween instead.[2]

Old World Traditions

In Poland and in German-speaking countries, it was the custom for children to dress up and beg for sweets at Christmastime.[3] The Germans who came to America also brought with them many tales of witches, as did the waves of people who came from Africa and Haiti. The French immigrants contributed the practice of "charivari," or "shivaree," the noisy playing of pranks.[4]

In Ireland, boys hunted down wrens—small, energetic birds—in celebration of St. Stephen's Day. They then wore costumes and went door to door asking for money. If the adult obliged, he or she was often given a feather from the wren for good luck.

The Victorian Halloween

In upper-class America in the Victorian era, Halloween was mainly a time for young, unmarried adults to have parties. Invitations sometimes arrived with jack-o'-lanterns or wrapped around tiny handmade witches. Many included rhymes such as this one:

> Come at the witching hour of eight
> And let the fairies read your fate;
> Reveal to none this secret plot
> Or woe—not luck—will be your lot![5]

Arriving at the party, guests found such cleverly crafted decorations as cobwebs made of yarn, hanging ghosts, and writhing tin snakes. Because the guests were usually unmarried, there were many fortune-telling and matchmaking games.[6]

Mischief Night

Like Halloween itself, Mischief Night has a long and varied past. In Halifax, Nova Scotia, Mischief Night was known as Cabbage-Stump Night because

Costumes in the early 1900s looked like this, as shown on the sheet music for "The Masquerade."

young people used the long cabbage stalks to bang on their neighbors' doors.[7] In Ireland, they filled the stalks with tow, a highly flammable plant material, set it on fire and blew the flames through keyholes.[8]

Back in the nineteenth century, kids would soap up windows to people's homes, tie doors shut, and tip over outhouses—sometimes with the occupant still inside! Another favorite Halloween trick was to hoist a farmer's wagon or buggy onto his rooftop.[9]

At first, the adults were amused by these pranks. They good-naturedly blamed them on witches, ghosts, and goblins. After all, it was Halloween. But sometimes things got out of hand. A Canadian rhyme from the late 1800s shows that people were losing patience with the rowdiness and destruction:

> Now the urchin hath his fun,
> The reign of terror's now begun,
> For Hallowe'en is here.[10]

After a while, the adults got the idea of bribing the neighborhood children. In America, by the 1930s, they were inviting the would-be pranksters inside for cider and donuts.[11] Homeowners found that when they attracted the kids with spooky decorations, then gave them something good to eat, the "little rowdies"[12] left their property alone.

There is a big difference between simple pranks and vandalism. Unfortunately, it is vandalism that marks the later development of Mischief Night in America. In Detroit, in 1984, there were 810 cases of arson, or deliberately set fires, over Mischief Night and Halloween. Halloween-related crimes were committed in New York and San Francisco too. Even outside the big cities, mailboxes were broken, cars were spray-painted, and tombstones were knocked over. Since the 1980s, there has been a decline in Halloween vandalism, thanks to neighborhood patrols and alternative activities like concerts and parties.[13] In England, Mischief Night is still celebrated on November 4 (the eve of Guy Fawkes Day), but in America it takes place either on Halloween itself or the night before.

Trick or Treat!

Halloween mischief, from smashed pumpkins to arson, still occurs. Parents and the police watch carefully for any signs of trouble and are quick to intervene. But for most children, mischief has been replaced by trick-or-treating.

When costumed children ring a doorbell, the first thing they say is the familiar phrase, "trick or treat." Today, however, very few trick-or-treaters are ready to perform a trick if they are refused a treat. They have likely forgotten the elaborate pranks played by previous generations. In 1972, the following rhyme was written down by a folklorist in Niagara Falls. It does not mention any threat to be mischievous if not given a treat.

> Trick or treat,
> Smell our feet.
> We want something
> Good to eat.[14]

But trick-or-treating is not only about dressing up and getting as much candy as possible. Since 1950, thousands of children across America have collected pennies for UNICEF. This charitable organization sends money to help children in need, worldwide.

Dressing Up

The practice of dressing in costumes for Halloween can be traced back to the early European festivals. People began to dress like the very witches, ghosts, and fairies that they feared. They performed short skits in return for food or drink. This practice of parading around in masks was called mumming. Dressing up in costumes—scary or not—has remained a favorite part of the holiday celebration.[15]

In America, as more and more children began trick-or-treating, costumes became a bigger and bigger part of Halloween. Over the years, these costumes have gone through several transformations. Starting out with witches, fairies, and bedsheet ghosts, the 1920s saw the arrival of burglars, cowboys and Indians, and gypsy girls. The discovery of King Tut's tomb made ancient Egyptian costumes all the rage in 1924, but mostly for adults.[16]

Hoboes and tramps were a common sight during the Great Depression of the 1930s, not just at Halloween, but in real life. Work was scarce, so many men took to the roads, often hopping freight trains to get from one place to another without having to pay. They carried their belongings in a bag slung over their shoulders. The hobo is still a fairly popular last-minute costume because it is so easy to put together. A bag of laundry tied to the end of a stick, and voilà!

In the 1940s, people's minds were on the very real horrors of World War II, so not much attention was paid to Halloween. But the end of the war and the 1950s brought a new flow of costumes inspired

The Great Depression

When stock prices began to fluctuate in September of 1929, there was little concern. The United States had enjoyed an economically prosperous decade and was convinced that the good times would continue. However, on October 24, 1929, called Black Thursday, people began to sell their stocks as quickly as possible. Prices dropped rapidly, and the market was buoyed for several days. But on Black Tuesday, October 29, 1929, another wave of mass-selling started the Great Crash. Between October 29 and November 13 over $30 billion vanished from the American economy.

The Great Depression would last into World War II, affecting the lives of nearly every American.

President Herbert Hoover was unable to provide the relief that the country sought. In an effort to combat the Depression, Americans elected Franklin Delano Roosevelt as President in 1932. Roosevelt brought with him a "New Deal" for Americans, which included relief programs and measures to increase employment as well as aid industrial and agricultural recovery from the Depression.

Roosevelt's programs helped to reorganize both the economy and the government, and began the process of slowly pulling America out of the Depression.

by the work of Walt Disney. Mickey Mouse and Tinkerbell were among the first.[17]

The influence of the movie industry continued on through the 1970s with costumes inspired by the *Star Wars* trilogy. Also, in the 1970s adults started to dress up again as they had in the early 1900s. Some put on costumes when they escorted their trick-or-treating children, but others did it just for fun. By 1980, one in four adults was dressing up for Halloween. It is now common to see adults dressed up in parades, at parties, and at work. Some people even dress up their pets.[18]

In the 1990s, elaborate historical costumes became especially popular. Since these kinds of costumes are expensive to buy and difficult to make, most of them are rented. President and first-lady costumes as well as characters from Shakespeare plays are favorites. Face masks of current political news makers are also big sellers each year. But despite these new ideas, the most popular uniform for trick-or-treaters—the one to stand the test of time—is the witch.[19]

Parties

Until the 1940s, Halloween parties were still mostly for adults. Halloween noisemakers, paper

Face masks are a popular costume. Some are scarier than others.

lanterns, and other decorations from the early decades of the twentieth century look a lot more sinister than what is around today. Those that survive are now collector's items. It was not until after World War II that black cats and jack-o-lanterns became cute so that children would not be afraid of them.[20]

Nowadays, many parents prefer their children to attend Halloween parties instead of walking the streets with their bags and knocking on the doors of unknown neighbors. This trend began in the 1970s after reports of drug-laced candy and razor blades in apples made parents fear for the safety of their little ghosts and witches. These events have become urban legends, and no one to date has found a razor blade in an apple, but they are repeated each year as if they were true. News-papers print tips on how to make sure the treats children bring home are safe.

Also unfounded are rumors of cult members who kidnap children on Halloween. These stories started to circulate in the late 1970s and early 1980s, increasing parents' fears.[21]

So if the stories are made up, why do they continue to be told? Probably for the same reason that people have always told scary stories on Halloween—just like lighting bonfires and setting

Urban Legends

Have you heard about my cousin's friend's sister, who was at a slumber party where a girl named Sally claimed that, earlier in the week, a man had been buried alive in the cemetery down the street? She said that it was still possible to hear him scratching at the lid of the coffin. The other girls did not believe her, and dared her to go down to the cemetery and drive a stake into the ground around the grave so that the next day they would know that she really went. Sally left and never returned. The others figured that she had just gotten scared and gone home. The next day the girls were passing the graveyard when they saw Sally lying on the ground by the grave. She had accidentally staked her sweater to the ground and when she tried to run away and could not, she died of fright.

These tall tales, known as urban legends, are stories that may have started with a grain of truth, but have been retold and exaggerated until becoming almost mythical. What gives urban legends more credibility is that they often happened to a friend of a friend of a friend, giving them some semblance of truth. Whether fact or fiction, urban legends tend to spread quickly and are generally believed to be true, though they rarely are.

out food for the dead, scary stories give us an acceptable way to express our doubts and fears.

These fears have done a lot to transform Halloween. Although there were Halloween parades and parties long before worries about poisoned treats and Halloween cults, the parades and parties took place in addition to trick-or-treating. Today, they are offered to children as a safe alternative. Trick-or-treating continues, but the cider and donuts of the 1930s have been replaced by packaged, manufactured candy. Most people have stopped handing out homemade treats because parents are afraid to let their children eat them.

Each year, Americans spend about $4 billion on Halloween costumes, decorations, and candy.[22]

Halloween and Hollywood

Today, when teenagers get together on Halloween, they do not turn over outhouses or watch for their true love's reflection in a candlelit mirror. Instead, they often sit down and watch a scary movie. Since the 1970s, October has been the season to release horror films, many of which have had a Halloween theme.

Movies in general have had a strong influence on Halloween. The animated witch in Disney's

Actor Bela Lugosi
played the evil
Count Dracula
in the 1931 movie.

1937 *Snow White and the Seven Dwarfs* introduced children to the image of witches as ugly old women.[23] And before the Wicked Witch of the West appeared dressed all in black in 1939's *The Wizard of Oz*, witches were just as likely to wear green, red, or blue.[24]

One of the most popular Halloween costumes ever manufactured was the mask worn by the killer in the trilogy of *Scream* movies.[25] Although the classic movie characters of Dracula, the Mummy, and the Wolf Man originally had nothing to do with Halloween, they have since come to represent the season.

Just as Hollywood has made its mark on Halloween, Halloween has also influenced Hollywood. For example, although there is no mention of Halloween or its symbols in Washington Irving's story "The Legend of Sleepy Hollow," the jack-o'-lantern is an important feature of the movie versions.[26]

In the fall of 1978, the low-budget horror movie *Halloween* was released. *Halloween* was the first in a series of films that featured all of the frightening rumors that were circulating at the time: human sacrifice, the targeting of innocent children by a crazed stranger, and even hidden razor blades. Audiences enjoyed *Halloween* so much that it remained the top-grossing independent film until 1999's *The Blair Witch Project*.[27] Other classic horror movies that continue to be shown at Halloween include *Don't Look Now* (1973), *Rosemary's Baby* (1968), and *The Exorcist* (1973).

Why do moviegoers like to watch their worst imaginings unfold on the screen? Mostly, people fear what is different or unknown. Much of the time, they try not to think about the things that frighten them. Scary movies, like ghost stories or tales about witches and goblins, help bring people's fears and worries out into the open. If, once in a while, we can scream out loud at them with other people, we feel better than if we keep our nightmares hidden inside.

Who Celebrates Halloween?

Halloween is a North American holiday, but it is both closely and distantly related to other festivals around the world. Some of these festivals are celebrated at harvest time, others in the spring and summer. They all honor the dead, some with great seriousness, others in a more lighthearted way. They also all make use of special foods, whether it is store-bought candy or homemade bread. Lights—candles, bonfires, or firecrackers—help the dead find their way home.

All Saints' and All Souls' Days

On All Saints' Day in France, it is traditional to clean the family graves. In Sweden, wreaths and candles are placed on the graves.[1] On the morning of November 2, Italians go to church where a mass is said for the souls of the dead. After church, the family graves are decorated with flowers and candles.[2] On the island of Sicily, children leave their shoes outside the door so they can be filled with presents. This is their reward for praying for the souls of the dead.[3]

In Rome, Italy's capital, All Souls' Day is a popular time for couples to announce they are getting married. The bride-to-be receives her engagement ring in a box filled with *fave dei morti.* Though the name means "beans of the dead," these are actually little cakes made of almonds, sugar, butter, and flour.[4]

In Mexico, All Souls' Day, celebrated on November 2, is known as *El Día de los Muertos,* or "Day of the Dead," and is a national holiday. November 1—called *El Día de los Santos* "day of the Saints"—is devoted to paying respects to the spirits of dead children, while November 2 honors the adult family members who have died.[5] Together, the two holidays are known as *Todos Santos,* or "All Saints."[6]

Before the Spanish arrived in Mexico in the sixteenth century, the native Aztecs and Mayans had many rituals that celebrated death as the other half of life. When the native peoples were forced to convert to Christianity, many of these rituals merged with the Catholic observance of All Souls.[7]

The Aztecs and Mayans

The Mayans were a successful civilization. The Mayan empire was spread out across southern Mexico and Central America, including the Yucatán Peninsula. The Mayan civilization peaked between A.D. 250 and 900, but was not officially conquered until the Spaniards arrived in the 1500s. The Mayans also thought that religion was very important, and worshipped more than 160 gods.

The Aztecs were another people who ruled a large and powerful empire in Mexico. The empire reached its height during the 1400s and 1500s, until it was conquered by Spaniards in 1521. Modern-day Mexico City sits on what was once Tenochtitlán, the Aztec capital city. Tenochtitlán was built on an island in a lake. According to legend, it was built in 1325. Religion was very important to the Aztecs, who worshipped hundreds of gods and goddesses.

Todos Santos honors not only the spirits of the dead, but death itself. Bakeries and market stalls offer chocolate hearses, sugar coffins and funeral wreaths, and marzipan skulls.[8] Graves and home altars are decorated with yellow marigolds, yellow being the ancient Mexican color of death.[9] At Todos Santos, death is not seen as a thing to be feared. Instead, it is celebrated as a natural part of life.

Preparations for the holiday begin on October 31 with cooking, cleaning, and candle making.[10] People bake *pan de muertos*, "bread of the dead," in fancy shapes. Altars called *ofrendas* are built in the home. Food, flowers, fruit, and sugar toys are laid on the altars for the spirits of the dead children. The spirits supposedly arrive around midnight while the family prays. The next morning, the children are allowed to eat what is left on the altar.

Larger ofrendas are set up the next day and piled with spicy food, clothing, alcohol, and even cigarettes. These are for the spirits of people who died as adults. Food, flowers, and candles are also taken to the family graves. During the day, there are picnics, parties, and music in the cemeteries, where it is believed the dead have returned to have a good time with their living relatives.[11]

Families stay in the cemeteries long into the night, burning candles to light the way for

Candy skulls are sold during Todos Santos.

returning souls. Fireworks and tolling bells also help the dead find their way through the night. It is important that no spirit is left to wander hungry and forgotten, because these ghosts may cause trouble for the living.[12]

Day of the Departed

In many Mexican-American communities, the Day of the Dead is known as *El Día de los Difuntos*, "Day of the Deceased," and *El Día de los Finados*, "Day of the Departed."[13] In places like Texas, New Mexico, and California, where there are large populations of Mexican Americans, pumpkins, Halloween candy, and black and orange balloons appear on graves and altars beside the more traditional flowers and candy skulls. In addition to yellow marigolds, the family graves are decorated with zinnias, coxcombs, and chrysanthemums as well as silk, plastic, and handmade paper flowers.[14]

The baking of pan de muertos is not as widespread in the American Southwest as it is in Mexico. The Mexican-American bakeries that do make it are as likely to shape their pan de muertos into bats, ghosts, and pumpkins as they are to bake it in the traditional shapes of human figures, bones, and skulls.[15]

Families make ofrendas, or altars, for their dead relatives. They adorn them with marigolds and items once treasured by the deceased.

Though some Mexican-American families do make ofrendas for their departed loved ones, the center of the celebration is the grave site. Often, family members journey from distant cities. When they arrive at the cemetery, they meet up with friends and relatives they have not seen all year. In this way, the Mexican-American All Souls is like a family reunion of the living as well as the dead.[16]

Images of Halloween witches and pumpkins have invaded the traditional Day of the Dead celebrations. At the same time, Day of the Dead is starting to make its mark on Halloween. Tourists from North America and other parts of the world travel to Mexico to view the candlelit graveyards and take part in the festivities of Todos Santos. In the United States, there have been many exhibits in museums and art galleries to teach people about the holiday.

Hungry Ghosts

China's Festival of the Hungry Ghosts is similar in many ways to both Halloween and Day of the Dead. Its celebration dates back to the sixth century A.D., but its origins may reach even farther back into prehistory.[17] Like Samhain and the Christian All Souls' Day, the Festival of the Hungry

During China's Festival of the Hungry Ghosts, people may burn offerings to pay their respects to their ancestors.

Ghosts, or *Chung Yuan*, is the time when the dead are believed to return to the earth.

The Chung Yuan Festival takes place during the last two weeks of the seventh lunar Chinese month, which falls around the same time as August and September. Family graves are tidied up and the spirits of the ancestors are given gifts of food, incense, and fake money, as well as paper copies of things they might have enjoyed in life.[18] These can include clothes, cars, horses, and furniture. Except for the food, all of these things must be burned so the dead will be able to use them.[19] During the Festival of the Hungry Ghosts, both Buddhist and Taoist priests perform ceremonies to help wandering spirits find their way to the afterlife.

The festival is not all grim. There are puppet shows and street operas, and children are allowed to gather up fallen candy after it is offered to the dead. Paper boats holding candles are floated on rivers and lakes, while flower-shaped lanterns are carried through the streets.

The Feast of Lanterns

Bon is another festival that has a lot in common with All Souls. Bon, also known as the Feast of Lanterns, is celebrated in Japan in July. Lights are placed at the gates of houses to help the souls of the dead find their way home.[20] Just like Halloween, Bon is the time for telling scary stories and thinking about the supernatural. A movie version of the famous *Yotsuya Ghost Story* is always shown on television at midnight during the Feast of Lanterns.

The main character of the *Yotsuya Ghost Story* is Oiwa, a beautiful young woman who was poisoned by her boyfriend. Several movies have been made about Oiwa, and each time there have been accidents, fires, and mechanical failures on the set. The only way to avoid such troubles, it is said, is for the cast and crew to pay a visit to Oiwa's grave.[21]

Walpurgis Night

The place where it is believed you can see the most witches in Europe, if not in the world, is the Harz Mountain region of Germany. But the so-called witches of the Harz come out on Walpurgis Night, April 30, instead of on Halloween.

April 30 is the eve of May Day, which was also the time the ancient Celts celebrated Beltane, the beginning of spring. In some Swedish villages, bonfires are lit on Walpurgis Night. It is said that if the flames blow north, spring will arrive slowly. If they blow toward the south, warm weather will come sooner.[22]

The holiday is named after Saint Walpurga whose one of four feast days is May 1, but the

These girls are dressed as witches during a parade in Germany.

original Walpurga may have been a pagan goddess.[23] In the Harz Mountains, people believed that witches flew through the sky on broomsticks, shovels, and pigs to gather on the highest peak on Walpurgis Night.[24] To scare the witches away, the locals banged on pots and pans, rang the church bells, and burned special herbs. Today in the villages of the Harz, schoolchildren dress up as devils and witches and parade through the streets on April 30. After dark, there are more parades of scary characters as well as outdoor plays, bonfires, and wilderness hikes.

The Spread of Halloween

In addition to Walpurgis Night, many German children have begun to celebrate Halloween, carving pumpkins and trick-or-treating American style, just like some Mexican children now celebrate both Halloween and Day of the Dead.[25] The American Halloween is also taking hold in France, threatening the more traditional ritual of grave cleaning on All Saints' Day.[26] The French do not celebrate in quite the same way as the Americans. The idea of trick-or-treating has not quite caught on in France. Since arriving in Paris in the 1990s, Halloween has been mainly an adult

Halloween has spread to many countries. This family sets up a Halloween display on their farm in Canada.

party night. Swedes, too, now enjoy carving pumpkins and hosting Halloween costume parties. But as in France, trick-or-treating has yet to become popular in Sweden.[27]

American Halloween images are now well enough known in Japan that they are used in advertisements there. Since Halloween occurs in the fall and is not considered a religious holiday in Japan, it will probably never become confused with the Bon Festival.[28]

Halloween has made a comeback in England, but instead of returning to the soul cakes of the old days, English children are celebrating the holiday by trick-or-treating, just like their American counterparts. Not everyone is happy about this worldwide trend. One Mexican writer has even called it "cultural pollution," viewing it as an affront to the more respectful Day of the Dead traditions.[29] And in Scotland, some people are upset to see pumpkins replacing turnip lanterns and American movie characters replacing local "ghosties and ghoulies" in store window displays.[30]

While Halloween means different things to different cultures, with its centuries-old symbolism, the holiday is clearly not going away any time soon.

Halloween Symbols

t would not be Halloween without bats and black cats, jack-o'-lanterns and apples, witches and ghosts, skeletons and candy. These are recognizable symbols of Halloween in most places around the world. Since Halloween is a mixture of two ancient traditions—celebrating harvest time and appeasing the souls of the dead—the symbols of the holiday have their roots in either one or both of those customs.

So how does an ordinary object like a pumpkin become a symbol of a holiday? Why are the colors black and orange the two colors everyone thinks of when they think of Halloween? There is a story behind each object that has come to represent this magical holiday.

Witches

A witch flying on a broomstick is perhaps the most recognizable symbol of the Halloween holiday. There have been dark times in history, both in Europe and in America, where innocent women (and some men) were accused of practicing witchcraft and put to death for it.[1] But these so-called witches were not always hated; although, they were usually feared.[2]

The word *witch* is derived from the old English word *wicca*, which means "wise one" or "wizard." Many people believed it was possible to bend the forces of nature to one's will. They believed that some women could cast real spells and use special potions to try to make things happen. People would ask these women for help if they needed something—for a crop to do well, a battle to end in their favor, or even for the object of their affection to fall in love with them.

Believe it or not, some of these women actually *did* ride broomsticks, although they were not flying in the air. As part of a ritual to encourage the land to be fruitful and the animals to multiply, women used to gather in large groups and ride on broomsticks or tree branches like they were riding on a horse.[3]

One of the times during the year that women held this special gathering was Halloween. The festivals were colorful celebrations, and both men and women were allowed to participate. There was dancing and music and it lasted long into the night.

In the United States, witchcraft is now recognized as a religion. More than a million Americans consider themselves to be witches, or Wiccans.[4] They

Witches are a favorite Halloween costume.

practice a nature-based religion and their rituals are based on the changing seasons.

Today's typical Halloween witch still reflects the older stereotypes of a witch. Witches are usually pictured as old women with gray straggly hair, long noses, pointed black hats, warts, and an evil disposition.

Black Cats

When we look at our cuddly and furry pets, it is hard to believe that people were ever scared or suspicious of cats. But in the dark, all cats look black and mysterious. They slink around soundlessly, and as a warning to predators, they will hiss and raise the fur on their backs. More than any other animal, cats have a long history of being associated with magic and death.

In ancient Egypt, the cat was the symbol of the Egyptians' beloved goddess Bast (or Pascht), who was the daughter of the sun god, Ra. Because of this, cats were worshiped too. They were considered so holy that they were often mummified alongside their owners.

In the Norse tradition, the goddess Freya was also known as the Mistress of Magic. She rode in a chariot pulled by cats to collect slain warriors to escort them to their resting place.

In the British Isles, the Celtic people feared cats and were often not very nice to them. They believed that cats used to be people who had been cursed. They also believed that witches could turn into cats themselves to carry out their evil plans. The black cat is often pictured at the side of a witch as her trusted companion because witches were thought to have evil sidekicks known as "familiars," who often took the shape of cats. Some thought that a cat was actually a witch in disguise.

During Samhain, cats were especially feared in case they were on a mission for a witch—or worse, the cat could be a witch itself. Samhain was not a safe time to be a cat. Even in America today, many animal shelters and pet stores will not sell black cats during the month of October.[5]

The black color of the cat, the witch's outfit, and bats—all are reminders that Halloween used to be a festival for the dead.

Bats

Before scientists understood much about animals and their behavior, the bat was a mystery. The bat does have some very unusual characteristics. It is the only mammal that can fly, and it is only seen flying in the dark of night. The fact that it can find its way around in the dark only adds to its mystique. During the day it hangs upside down in caves with its wings wrapped around its body like a witch's cape. The tiny furry face of the bat can look very scary with its long ears and pointy teeth.

Bats hang upside down and are quite scary-looking.

Long ago it was believed that witches would rub the blood of bats onto their skin before they practiced magic.[6] The women would then dance around bonfires, and bats could be seen flying overhead. This gave people even more reason to associate bats and witches. But bats eat moths, and moths are attracted to the fire, so it was likely not the witches who the bats came to see.

Then, of course, there is the vampire bat. These bats are not just in Hollywood movies—there really is a vampire bat that lives in Central and South America. It survives by drinking the blood of other animals. Luckily for all involved, the vampire bat is not known to go after humans, and it does not turn into a vampire.

Jack-O'-Lantern

The carved-out pumpkin with the grinning face and the candle inside comes from a combination of historical elements. In the British Isles, there are a lot of swamps, marshes, and bogs. Sometimes, at night, a faint light would appear to swirl in the air above them. This was likely a natural by-product of the animal and plant life that was disintegrating in the murky water, but to the people who saw it, it looked like a ghost was wandering through the swamps with a lantern.

According to Irish folklore, the most famous swamp traveler was a man named Jack who tricked the Devil so many times that he was banned from both heaven and hell. Jack was doomed to walk the earth forever, with just the light of a single ember to guide him through the darkness. He supposedly found a hollowed-out vegetable and placed his ember inside it.[7]

Jack-o'-lanterns can be scary or friendly.

Since the tradition of walking from door to door on Halloween took place at night, the people needed a lantern to guide the way and to protect them from harm by keeping the evil spirits away. The type of vegetable that travelers used varied according to what crops were produced in that country.

In Ireland they used potatoes, in Scotland they used turnips, and in England they used large beets. When the Halloween tradition came to America, the people discovered that pumpkins were the perfect replacement. Pumpkins were much easier to hollow out than beets or turnips.[8] With the advent of electricity and streetlights, trick-or-treaters did not actually have to carry the pumpkins from house to house, but rather left them on their front porch where they stood as a symbol of the spirit world.

Carving faces in pumpkins gives them an even eerier look. This tradition likely began in America in the late nineteenth century. The orange color of the pumpkin represents the fall colors of the annual harvest of fruit, vegetables, and grains that takes place at this time of the year.

Ghosts and Skeletons

In the earliest days of Halloween, many people believed that the souls of the dead could visit the land of the living. They believed their dead relatives would come back to their houses looking for a comfortable home for the night.[9] People would lay out tables of food in the hopes of pleasing the ghosts and assuring that the ghosts would not hurt them or steal from them. They also prayed for their dead relatives who might be stuck in purgatory—the place that they believed lies between heaven and hell. They hoped that by praying for them, they would be allowed into heaven.

Many people think of skeletons and skulls when Halloween is mentioned. Spooky skulls can be used to decorate houses.

People believed it was during this time of year that the veil separating the world of the living from the world of the dead is the thinnest.[10] The bones of the dead—a skeleton—is a good symbol for this special time, because it is not alive, yet it used to be. It is very strange to think we all carry around a skeleton inside our bodies.

Halloween Food: Candy, Apples, and Nuts

Who can imagine Halloween without candy corn, those tasty triangles of sugar that look like pieces of corn? Candy corn is a symbol of the times when the holiday celebrated the harvest. But we give candy to trick-or-treaters for another reason too. On Halloween night, people used to give poor people sweets so that they would pray for the souls of the dead, thereby giving the wealthier people a greater chance at getting their relatives into heaven.[11]

Apples and nuts are a symbol of a fruitful harvest too. People give apples to trick-or-treaters, and they also include them in games, such as bobbing for apples in big tins of water. Historically these items revolved around predicting the future, especially young people's search for love. If they

When one sees candy corn in the stores, then Halloween must be around the corner.

caught the apple in their teeth, they would marry their true love. Young people would place a pair of nuts in the fire and if they cracked and rolled apart, then the relationship was doomed.[12]

Some of these games are still played, but most have been lost to time. New traditions have risen up in their place, which is only fitting for a holiday that keeps growing and changing every year.

How Halloween Is Celebrated Today

Halloween in America is not just trick-or-treating anymore. The celebrations take many shapes and forms. Depending on where in the United States you live, or how scared you want to be, you may spend your Halloween at a pumpkin-carving party, marching in a parade, riding on a haunted hayride, or visiting a haunted house.

Halloween has also become a time for honoring interesting figures in American culture. Edgar

Allan Poe was known for his ghoulish horror stories, and each year in Baltimore, poems are recited at his candlelit grave. In Washington, D.C., the memory of magician Harry Houdini, who died on Halloween, is honored at a Black Magic Ball.[1] While celebrations are held in cities and towns of all sizes, three cities in America truly transform on Halloween—New York, New York; Salem, Massachusetts; and New Orleans, Louisiana.

New York: The Village Halloween Parade

On Halloween 1973, a man named Ralph Lee founded the Greenwich Village Halloween Parade.[2] Lee was a puppeteer, mask maker, and theater director who wanted to share his talent with his community. The first parade was made up of one hundred and fifty of Lee's acquaintances. They dressed up in mythical costumes or worked giant puppets Lee had designed and created. The parade was led by a group of women who dressed like witches and walked on stilts while sweeping the pavement with twig brooms.

In the beginning, it took only about an hour for the parade to wind its way through Greenwich Village's historic district to end in Washington Square Park. Most of the spectators lived nearby,

The Halloween parade in New York City attracts many people. This skeleton puppet makes its way down the street.

or had discovered the parade by accident. But each year the parade got more elaborate as more and more people heard about it and came to watch. By the 1980s, thousands were marching in the parade and hundreds of thousands were coming to watch.[3] The event outgrew the narrow streets where it had started and had to be moved to Sixth Avenue.

The costumes in the parade have gotten very creative. Costumes seen in the last decade include a tube of toothpaste, a cornflake, a gas pump, and an already-chewed piece of gum. Groups of friends have dressed as a roach motel, a human clothes-line, and a broken-down subway car.[4] And it is not just the marchers who dress up. Most of the spectators and even the police who control the crowd are also in costume.

With so many people, it now takes about five hours to complete the route. The Village Halloween Parade is not a quiet event either. There is music from mariachi, reggae, and klezmer bands, and the crowd makes a lot of noise cheering and clapping for the marchers.

Halloween in New Orleans

New Orleans is the unofficial capital of voodoo in America. Voodoo, also called vodoun or vodun, is a religion that blended West African religion with Caribbean French Catholicism. It involves a belief in magic and witches, and involves worshiping ancestors believed to hold power over the living.[5] It came to America from Cuba and Haiti. At New Orleans' Voodoo Museum, visitors can look in on real voodoo rituals. There is even a Halloween Voodoo Ritual Lunch in the city each year.[6] Bourbon Street in New Orleans has always been the main site for the city's annual Halloween Parade. Halloween 2005 was no exception. In a city torn apart only weeks before by Hurricane Katrina, celebrating Halloween in true New Orleans style gave many people a much needed break.

The big old houses in historical New Orleans have always made excellent haunted houses. Many houses claim their own ghosts and offer tours, one of which includes a ghost train and haunted hayride where the spooks who jump out of the bushes to scare the passengers are actually costumed policemen. New Orleans has also become the site of a famous vampire costume party inspired by the books of local horror writer Anne Rice. Each year tourists, locals, and actors dress up as characters from New Orleans history. The history of this thriving, energetic city is now being rewritten, and the Halloween costumes will no doubt follow.

Salem: The Witch City

Another city famous for its Halloween celebrations is Salem, Massachusetts. The Puritans, who founded Salem Village in the seventeenth century, were Protestants from England. They did not celebrate Hallowtide (as the holiday was called back then) because they thought of it as a Catholic tradition. But although they did not believe in Halloween, they certainly believed in witches. From 1691 to 1692, nineteen women, one man, and one dog were put to death for the crime of practicing witchcraft.[7]

While there was no proof that any of these people were actually witches, a belief in witchcraft gave the citizens of Salem a focus for their fears. If a crop failed, a young girl had a seizure, a cow stopped giving milk, or a baby died, it was easier to blame the woman next door than to look for another reason for their bad luck.

The Puritans of Salem were not the first people to accuse their neighbors of witchcraft. There had been witch trials in Europe since around the fifteenth century. In the sixteenth and seventeenth centuries, several *thousand* people, mostly women, were put to death as witches.

In the 1970s, Salem became known as the "Witch City." Because of its history of witchcraft, many modern day witches (or Wiccans) had settled there.[8] Thousands of tourists started to arrive on Halloween, and in 1981, the Salem Witch Museum hosted its first Haunted Happenings celebration. At first, it was only a one-day event, but since then it has grown into a month-long city wide festival. During the month of October, the quarter of a million visitors to the Witch City can visit the Salem Wax Museum; take the Haunted Footsteps Tour, "Salem's Official Ghostly Tour" or walk the Terror Trail, a spooky, candlelit journey.[9] For those more interested in Salem's historical background, there is the Witch Trial Trail, Salem Witch Museum, Witch History Museum, and Salem spirits of 1692 Trolley Tour. The Witches' League for Public Awareness sponsors a series of lectures to educate the public about modern Wiccans.[10]

Not surprisingly, Salem also has plenty of haunted houses to choose from. There is the Hall of Illusions, the Haunted Witch Village, and the famous House of Seven Gables, which was the setting for a novel by Nathaniel Hawthorne. Written in 1851, *The House of the Seven Gables* is the story

The House of Seven Gables was the setting for
a novel by Nathaniel Hawthorne.

of the Pyncheons, a family living under a curse. Hawthorne was probably inspired by his own family history. His great-great grandfather, John Hathorne, was one of the judges who condemned many innocent women to death during the Salem Witch Trials. Nathaniel Hawthorne added the *w* to his last name to distance himself from the terrible deeds of his ancestor. His family believed themselves cursed because of what their ancestor did, even though it was actually the local reverend who one of the victims—Sara Good—cursed with her last breath.[11]

Haunted houses give people the chance to feel safe while they are being scared. But what many people think of as the ultimate haunted house is much newer and is not in Salem.

Haunted Houses

Walt Disney first got the idea for his Haunted Mansion in 1951, but it took so much work to build that it was not finished until 1969. Disney used all the cutting-edge technology and special effects of the time to create a ghost train, graveyard, séance parlor, stone statues that come to life, and a ballroom full of dancing spirits. You can see versions of the Haunted Mansion at Disneyland,

Walt Disney World, Tokyo Disney, and Disneyland Paris.[12]

The Haunted Mansion is open year-round, but if you want to make your own haunted house, it is more convenient to do it for just one night of the year. What better night than Halloween? Inspired by amusement park fun houses, homeowners started creating their own Halloween haunted houses in the 1930s and 1940s. It was not hard to do. They simply turned out all the lights and let their guests handle peeled grapes, cold pasta, and poultry giblets, telling them they were human body parts.

Since the 1970s, haunted houses have also been used as fund-raisers by charitable organizations like the Jaycee's, a community volunteer organization, and March of Dimes, whose mission is to improve the health of babies. Community centers, city parks, and barns are also popular places for hauntings during the Halloween season.

Many children like to decorate their family's front yard for Halloween. With some paint and foam, you can turn the front yard into a graveyard without much time or money.

But there are some families who are willing to spend the time and money on a really elaborate display. They use equipment such as film projectors, fog machines, and strobe lights to make the lawn look scary in the dark. Some rig up "flying ghosts" on wires and play eerie sound effects.

For people who decorate their lawns, Halloween provides a chance to create something special and often to become a local celebrity, at least for a day. It also helps people feel connected to their communities because children and adults they might not otherwise talk to come to admire their creations.

Other Halloween Options

Not all Halloween celebrations are spooky. One example of a nonscary event is an annual pumpkin-carving party in Granville, Ohio. It began as a party for eight, but soon grew to eighty and is now a community event with activities for both children and grown-ups. In addition to the actual carving, which is done by the adults, there is also paint, pipe cleaners, and other craft materials for

Instead of trick-or-treating, some cities hold pumpkin-carving contests.

the children, and a potluck supper. Once the pumpkins are carved, the pulp that is scooped out is recycled on the compost heap.[13]

Most public schools have Halloween parades and parties, but many now have strict rules about what kinds of costumes students are allowed to wear. It is not surprising that weapons or costumes with violent themes are forbidden. But some schools even ban witches, ghosts, and devils.[14] In Iowa City, in 1993, students were discouraged from dressing up as gypsies, Native Americans, Africans, witches, or old people, among other things, because the school feared someone might be offended.[15]

In some towns, malls offer Halloween parades and trick-or-treating because enclosed shopping centers are supposedly safer than children's own neighborhoods. Parents can either drop off their children, or wait while the kids collect candy, play games, and compete in costume contests. "Safe" trick-or-treating is offered not just in malls, but in community centers, police stations, and office buildings.[16]

For many reasons, some people still view Halloween as a threat. Some think it should not be celebrated in public because they think it is a religious holiday. Others think of it as a satanic or

Some people bake cookies in spooky Halloween shapes for parties.

pagan ritual. Some adults think of Halloween as a chance for children to get into or cause trouble.

There has been a lot of effort to control Halloween. In the state of Maryland, a campaign was started to make Halloween the last Saturday of October every year. Since this is still daylight savings time, fewer children would be out in the dark, and Halloween would never fall on a school night.[17] Some religious activists have asked school boards to ban Halloween celebrations altogether.[18]

Despite these efforts, Halloween survives and even thrives. For a hundred years, it has been a nationwide celebration despite the fact that it is not an official national holiday like Thanksgiving or Christmas. It definitely has its commercial aspects with the sales of candy, costumes, decorations, greeting cards, and the like. But for most people, Halloween is a time of magic and make-believe.

On Halloween, we can be anything we want to be. For one day a year, we can pretend to be ballerinas, firemen, doctors, werewolves, or anything else we can dream up. What a great way to express ourselves (and get some candy at the same time)!

Paper "Jack-O'-Lantern"

You will need:

- ✔ pencil
- ✔ paper cup
- ✔ light cardboard
- ✔ scissors
- ✔ clear tape

- ✔ orange tissue paper
- ✔ yellow tissue paper
- ✔ white tissue paper
- ✔ pipe cleaner

What you will do:

1 Trace the bottom of a paper cup onto a piece of light cardboard. Cut out the circle.

2 Place a large sheet of orange tissue paper on your workspace. Stick loops of clear tape to the circle and place it, tape side down, in the center of the orange tissue paper.

3 Use a pencil to mark the jack-o'-lantern's face. The bottom of the mouth should be about 1½ inches above the circle. Draw a mouth, eyes, and nose. Carefully cut out the mouth, eyes, and nose.

4 Cut a piece of yellow tissue paper large enough to cover the cutout face. Tape the yellow tissue paper down with clear tape.

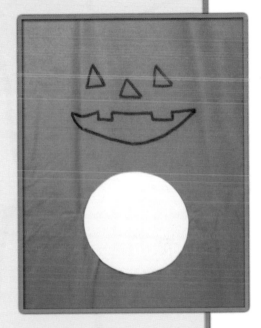

5 Loosely crumple two or three pieces of white tissue paper and place them on the cardboard circle.

6 Bring up the orange tissue paper and smooth the face in front of the white tissue paper. Fold the sides up, and smooth back. Gather the back of the orange tissue paper and bring to the top. Use a pipe cleaner to tie around the top.

Decorate your house for Halloween or make more to give to friends!

GLOSSARY

alternative—The choice between two possibilities.

ancestor—A person from whom one is descended, more remote or distant than a grandparent.

appease—To bring peace, quiet, or calm to; soothe.

convert—To persuade another to adopt a particular religion, faith, or belief.

cult—A religious sect generally considered to be extremist or false.

hearse—A vehicle for carrying a coffin to a funeral or cemetery.

hearth—The floor of a fireplace, usually extending into a room and paved with brick, stone, or cement.

ritual—The performance of acts as in a religious ceremony.

séance—A gathering of people to receive messages from beyond the grave.

stereotype—A generalized way of thinking about members of a certain group that represents an oversimplified opinion, or a prejudiced attitude.

symbol—Something that stands for, or suggests, something else.

tradition—The passing down of the practices of a culture from one generation to the next.

vandalism—Willful destruction of public or private property.

CHAPTER NOTES

◆ Chapter 2. The History of Halloween

1. Nicholas Rogers, *Halloween: From Pagan Ritual to Party Night* (New York: Oxford University Press, 2002), p. 11.
2. Anthony Aveni, *The Book of the Year: A Brief History of Our Seasonal Holidays* (New York: Oxford University Press, 2003), p. 127.
3. Silver Ravenwolf, *Halloween: Customs, Recipes and Spells* (St. Paul, Minn.: Llewellyn Publications, 1999), p. 6.
4. Lesley Pratt Bannatyne, *Halloween: An American Holiday, An American History* (New York: Facts on File, 1990), p. 4.
5. Ibid., p. 2.
6. Aveni, p. 128.
7. Sir James George Frazer, *The Golden Bough* (New York: Collier Books, 1922), p. 735.
8. Aveni, p. 129.
9. David Skal, *Death Makes a Holiday: A Cultural History of Halloween* (New York: Bloomsbury, 2002), p. 22.
10. Rogers, pp. 27–28.
11. Skal, p. 23.
12. Rogers, p. 29.

13. Bannatyne, *Halloween: An American Holiday*, p. 6.
14. Sue Ellen Thompson, *Holiday Symbols*, 2nd ed. (Detroit: Omnigraphics, 2000), p. 208.
15. Skal, p. 24.
16. Tad Tuleja, "Trick-or-Treat: Pre-Texts and Contexts," in Jack Santino, *Halloween and Other Festivals of Death and Life* (Knoxville: University of Tennessee Press, 1994), pp. xv–xvi.
17. Rogers, p. 32.
18. Frazer, p. 736.
19. Rogers, p. 32.
20. Bannatyne, *Halloween: An American Holiday*, p. 73.

◆ Chapter 3. The Cultural Significance of Halloween

1. Tad Tuleja, "Trick-or-Treat: Pre-Texts and Contexts," in Jack Santino, *Halloween and Other Festivals of Death and Life* (Knoxville: University of Tennessee Press, 1994), p. 85.
2. David Skal, *Death Makes a Holiday: A Cultural History of Halloween* (New York: Bloomsbury, 2002), p. 46.
3. Tuleja/Santino, p. 84.
4. Steve Siporin, "Halloween Pranks: 'Just a Little Inconvenience'," in Jack Santino, *Halloween and Other Festivals of Death and Life* (Knoxville: University of Tennessee Press, 1994), pp. 50–51.

5. Lesley Pratt Bannatyne, *Halloween: An American Holiday, An American History* (New York: Facts on File, 1990), p. 111.

6. Skal, pp. 36–37.

7. Russell W. Belk, "Carnival, Control, and Corporate Culture in Contemporary Halloween Celebrations," in Jack Santino, *Halloween and Other Festivals of Death and Life* (Knoxville: University of Tennessee Press, 1994), p. 111.

8. Skal, p. 33.

9. Siporin/Santino, p. 48.

10. Nicholas Rogers, *Halloween: From Pagan Ritual to Party Night* (New York: Oxford University Press, 2002), p. 58.

11. Tuleja/Santino, p. 89.

12. Skal, p. 53.

13. Leslie Pratt Bannatyne, *A Halloween How-To* (Gretna, La.: Pelican Publishing, 2001), p. 231.

14. Hennig Cohen and Tristram Potter Coffin, eds., *The Folklore of American Holidays*, first ed. (Detroit: Gale Research Company, 1987), pp. 309–310.

15. Jack Santino, *All Around the Year: Holidays and Celebrations in American Life* (Champaign, Ill.: University of Illinois Press, 1995), p. 150.

16. Skal, p. 42.

17. Bannatyne, *A Halloween How-To*, p. 53.

18. Ibid., p. 53–54.

19. Ibid.

20. Marie Proeller Hueston, "Tricky Treats," *Country Living*, October 2004, pp. 70–72.

21. Bill Ellis, "'Safe' Spooks: New Halloween Traditions in Response to Sadism Legends," in Jack Santino, *Halloween and Other Festivals of Death and Life* (Knoxville: University of Tennessee Press, 1994), p. 25.

22. Skal, p. 57.

23. Bannatyne, *Halloween: An American Holiday*, pp. 136–137.

24. Skal, p. 39.

25. Ibid., p. 179.

26. Ibid., p. 160.

27. Ibid., p. 162.

◆ Chapter 4. Who Celebrates Halloween?

1. Lesley Pratt Bannatyne, *Halloween: An American Holiday, An American History* (New York: Facts on File, 1990), p. 236.

2. Sue Ellen Thompson and Barbara W. Carlson, eds., *Holidays, Festivals, and Celebrations of the World Dictionary* (Detroit: Omnigraphics, Inc., 1994), p. 7.

3. Ibid.

4. Ibid.

5. David Skal, *Death Makes a Holiday: A Cultural History of Halloween* (New York: Bloomsbury, 2002), p. 185.

6. Nicholas Rogers, *Halloween: From Pagan Ritual to Party Night* (New York: Oxford University Press, 2002), p. 144.

7. Rosemary Ellen Guiley, *The Encyclopedia of Ghosts and Spirits* (New York: Facts on File, 1992), p. 86.

8. Ibid.

9. Ibid.

10. Ibid.

11. Skal, p. 185.

12. Guiley, p. 86.

13. Kay Turner and Pat Jasper, "Day of the Dead: The Tex-Mex Tradition," in Jack Santino, *Halloween and Other Festivals of Death and Life* (Knoxville: University of Tennessee Press, 1994), p. 139.

14. Ibid., pp. 142–143.

15. Ibid., pp. 146–147.

16. Ibid., p. 140.

17. Sue Ellen Thompson, *Holiday Symbols*, 2nd ed. (Detroit: Omnigraphics, 2000), pp. 239–240.

18. *Chase's Calendar of Events, 2004* (Chicago: Contemporary Books/McGraw-Hill, 2004), p. 446.

19. Thompson, p. 240.

20. Guiley, p. 85.

21. Catrien Ross, *Supernatural and Mysterious Japan* (Tokyo: Yenbooks, 1996), pp. 157–158.

22. Thompson, p. 639.

23. Steenie Harvey, "Walpurgisnacht: Shrieks and Spooks in Schierke," *German Life*, April/May 2000, p. 24.

24. Andrea Schulte-Peevers, "Witches, Trains, and Half Timber—The Magic of the Harz," *German Life*, April/May 1996, p. 34.
25. Rogers, pp. 141–142.
26. Mark Abley, *Spoken Here: Travels among Threatened Languages* (Boston: Houghton Mifflin Company, 2003), p. 137.
27. Leslie Pratt Bannatyne, *A Halloween How-To* (Gretna, La.: Pelican Publishing, 2001), p. 236.
28. Skal, p. 152.
29. Rogers, p. 141.
30. Bannatyne, *A Halloween How-To*, p 236.

Chapter 5. Holiday Symbols

1. Silver Ravenwolf, *Halloween: Customs, Recipes and Spells* (St. Paul, Minn.: Llewellyn Publications, 1999), pp. 17–18.
2. Leslie Pratt Bannatyne, *A Halloween How-To* (Gretna, La.: Pelican Publishing, 2001), p. 225.
3. Sue Ellen Thompson, *Holiday Symbols*, 2nd ed. (Detroit: Omnigraphics, 2000), p. 210.
4. Ravenwolf, p. 63.
5. David Skal, *Death Makes a Holiday: A Cultural History of Halloween* (New York: Bloomsbury, 2002), p. 148.
6. Sue Ellen Thompson and Barbara W. Carlson, eds., *Holidays, Festivals, and Celebrations of the World Dictionary* (Detroit: Omnigraphics, Inc., 1994), p. 165.
7. Skal, p. 31.

8. Ibid., p. 35.
9. Jack Santino, *Halloween and Other Festivals of Death and Life* (Knoxville: University of Tennessee Press, 1994), p. xv.
10. Skal, p. 20.
11. Nicholas Rogers, *Halloween: From Pagan Ritual to Party Night* (New York: Oxford University Press, 2002), p. 28.
12. Anthony Aveni, *The Book of the Year: A Brief History of Our Seasonal Holidays* (New York: Oxford University Press, 2003), p. 126.

◆ Chapter 6. How Halloween Is Celebrated Today

1. Lesley Pratt Bannatyne, *Halloween: An American Holiday, An American History* (New York: Facts on File, 1990), p. 157.
2. David Skal, *Death Makes a Holiday: A Cultural History of Halloween* (New York: Bloomsbury, 2002), pp. 125–126.
3. Nicholas Rogers, *Halloween: From Pagan Ritual to Party Night* (New York: Oxford University Press, 2002), p. 134.
4. Ibid., pp. 129–131.
5. Bannatyne, *Halloween: An American Holiday*, pp. 85–86.
6. "Haunted New Orleans: Halloween Events Calendar, October 2004," n.d., <http://www.nola.com/haunted/?/haunted/content/hcalendar.html> (August 16, 2005).

7. Skal, p. 65.

8. Ibid., p. 73.

9. *Haunted Happenings*, Office of Tourism and Cultural Affairs (Salem, Mass.: Kishgraphics, 2004).

10. Bannatyne, *Halloween: An American Holiday*, p. 157.

11. Skal, p. 70.

12. Ibid., pp. 87–88.

13. Julia Szabo, "Pumpkin Party!" *Country Living*, October 2004, pp. 85–88.

14. Leslie Pratt Bannatyne, *A Halloween How-To* (Gretna, La.: Pelican Publishing, 2001), p. 245.

15. Skal, p. 142.

16. Bannatyne, *A Halloween How-To*, p. 246.

17. Ibid., p. 247.

18. Rogers, p. 12.

FURTHER READING

Barth, Edna. *Witches, Pumpkins, and Grinning Ghosts: The Story Of The Halloween Symbols.* New York: Clarion Books, 2000.

Galembo, Phyllis. *Dressed for Thrills: 100 Years of Halloween Costumes and Masquerade.* New York: Harry N. Abrams, 2002.

Greene, Carol. *The Story of Halloween.* New York: HarperCollins, 2004.

Jackson, Ellen. *The Autumn Equinox: Celebrating the Harvest.* Brookfield, Conn.: Millbrook Press, 2000.

Robinson, Fay. *Halloween Crafts.* Berkeley Heights, N.J.: Enslow Publishers, Inc., 2004.

White, Linda. *Haunting on a Halloween: Frightful Activities for Kids.* Salt Lake City, Utah: Gibbs Smith, 2002.

INTERNET ADDRESSES

Halloween.com
  <http://www.halloween.com>
  Learn even more about Halloween.

Holiday Fun: Happy Halloween
  <http://www.kidsdomain.com/holiday/
    halloween/>
  Find costume ideas, safety tips, and more at this site.

INDEX